For MaryAnn Handy (Gangy)

And Jewell Handy, my mother.

Part one

The Resistance

I

Ashley

This is a story of how the Demigod Resistance wanted a democracy instead of the tyrants, Tartarus and her, and how they fought for what they believed in. Before I tell you the story, I should introduce myself. My name is Ashley Brown, I'm a daughter of Athena, and I was the leader of the resistance. This is unlike any mortal one. For example instead of guns we use swords, knifes, and arrows for the time being, that is. We also don't use regular steel; instead we use a mixture of steel and bronze. This alloy or combination of metals is fatal to monsters. The resistance, like its name describes, is made up of demigods. A demigod is a child of a god or goddess. My brother, Alex Brown, and I are demigods. We are the children of Athena. My brother is kinda cute, with blonde hair, and brown eyes, which are the exact color of chocolate. He also is a really good strategist. He helps me plan all the raids and attacks against the ones who run the mythical realm, Tartarus and Hera.

Now when Tartarus and Hera took over we were very unprepared. Few had the supplies needed to survive; luckily we had our headquarters ready for something like this. We had weapons, food, and water. We had enough for an entire legion, a hundred people, to survive for three months. For the seven of us it was more than enough for a few years.

Sadly, monster attacks were frequent enough: so few had enough sleep. The Minotaur and hydras attacked almost every other day. A Minotaur is half man and half bull. Hydras are dragons with seven heads, and the middle one shoots fire. During these attacks those who could not fight well were vulnerable. Calypso, the daughter of Atlas, is one of those people. The attacks caused

Calypso to be caught by Medusa. Alex blames himself, but no one would have been able to stop Medusa from taking Calypso. Soon after, Alex was distraught. Every day he wanted to go find her and bring her back. So I quickly said, "Gather volunteers. Once you have one other than me we can plan a strategy to get Calypso back without anyone getting hurt."

___Soon after, Alex came back murmuring, "I have to be the one who goes with Ashley to help Calypso. I have to be." I became worried about my brother. He was acting very strange, and two days after I asked him to get a volunteer he asked if he could go on the mission to bring Calypso back. So I quickly replied, "Of course you can. Have you been getting ready, packing, and practicing your swordplay?" He whispered, "No, I haven't. In all my worrying I somehow forgot to practice. I'll practice tonight."

I merely nodded, for he knew that he was going to practice with Jason Holly, our top sword master and warrior. Soon after midnight, three hours later, Jason came in hardly sweating and said hoarsely, "Alex is ready, but I suggest keeping an eye on him." So I replied in kind, as I had not had a drink in a while, "He has had a lot on his mind. Thank you for practicing with him while I finished the paperwork that comes with a mission." Jason then left the room to go and practice on his own. I knew that he was uncomfortable with others so I let him leave. As he left I felt as though I should say something to him, so I asked, "Do you want to go and have some real practice?" Jason simply shook his head, and then left. I really was confused at this as normally Jason, being a son of Ares, would have loved to go and kill some monsters.

II

Alex

Now when Jason finished practicing with me I returned to my room, set my alarm for six a.m., and packed my bags so that I was ready to go in the morning. Though worried for Calypso's safety, I tried to get some sleep, but I sadly couldn't rest until she was safe and well. I would never tell my sister or anyone else but I have a crush on Calypso, but how do you ask out an immortal demigod? I mean seriously how do you? It's almost impossible to ask an immortal out. They almost always say no because of age difference.

But soon after tossing and turning for about an hour, I went and asked my sister, "What all is guarding Calypso?" My sister, Ashley, replied kindly, "I know that Medusa, Hydras, and the Minotaur are guarding her." Uh oh, Medusa, great just great. Why did it have to be Medusa guarding her, really why Medusa? I am still going after Calypso no matter what. Then I thought, this is going to be a little hard to rescue Calypso now that Medusa is involved.

Then, finally as the sun rose at six a.m., Ashley came and said quietly, "Time to go, we need to be able to surprise Medusa. Let's go." As we rode upon Pegasus, which are winged horses, we got to the headquarters of Hera and Tartarus within hours. As we passed over the country to get to Santa Fe, New Mexico we saw a desert, the Grand Canyon, and other amazing monuments. We knew that as we passed over these places we had to be careful so that mortals did not see us. The sights as we flew over were spectacular. Mortals think that airplanes get good views; well they should try Pegasus aerial views sometime. We got at Hera and Tartarus's camp shortly before nine a.m. Hera, unfortunately, had planned for someone to come after

Calypso, so she had many guards surrounding her. There were Cyclops, Medusa, Hydras, and the Minotaur. They were all armed to the teeth especially the hydras, which spit acid and shoot fire from their middle heads. As Ashley and I came closer we noticed that Calypso, who has brown hair, and gorgeous blue eyes, was well and safe, and she didn't try to escape. Then moments later she spotted us, perched over the camp as we were.

We sent the Pegasus into the monster's camp, so that they were distracted. Slowly we went into the camp, unlocked Calypso's cage and slowly sneaked to the back of the camp. There were five Hydras, the Minotaur, and Medusa, waiting for us. Of course they were. Medusa, as to not petrify us, wore sunglasses. The Hydras advanced, Ashley yelled to me, "Protect Calypso, keep her safe!" She pulled out her sword; dodging blasts of fire from the Hydras. She advanced even further by killing two of the Hydras. She was eventually burnt thrice by a single Hydra. While she fell I left Calypso defenseless so that I could protect my sister. I was knocked aside by the Minotaur. It then threw Ashley about fifty miles, where she landed heavily in a desert. It turned its attention to me. I fought with all my strength but in the end I was knocked unconscious. Ten minutes later I woke up and found myself tied up in front of Hera, who is one of the rulers of this realm. She then slapped me and yelled in a fury, "You decided to try your luck at rescuing your friend. Now I have lost two Hydras, some of my best warriors. I had hoped that you would wait a little longer to attack. Sadly, you didn't. No matter. Ashley is wounded and you have been captured. You have no hope, so tell me where your headquarters are and I will let you and your friends live." I sat there defiantly, staying silent to protect Ashley and the resistance.

When she realized I wouldn't tell her, Hera swiftly knocked me unconscious and I was carried into the main building, where I was locked inside.

III

Calypso

Sadly, as Ashley and Alex's plan to help me escape failed. The results were Alex was taken captive, and Ashley was gravely injured. I have been inside Tartarus and Hera's camp for three weeks now. Those three weeks have been the worst of my life and I have had a very long and dangerous life, as I am Atlas's daughter. I believe that my wardens have been warned to not harm me, as I have yet not been harmed at all. The time that I have spent here, at this camp, has not been very pleasant nor have my captors wanted it to be.

My captors wish for my spirit to be broken. Ha! Well they should know that as I have suffered greater disappointment, than not being rescued, that my spirit shall not be broken for a long, long time. Soon I realized that my captors wished not for my spirit to be broken, but instead they wanted to capture and kill the resistance. Thankfully my captors don't know that they shall never kill the resistance; instead, the resistance will kill them.

Ten minutes later Alex woke up. He inquired where he was. I replied

in a whisper, "In the main building."
He realized that we wouldn't get out
of here anytime soon. After that for
a few minutes we sat in silence. They
came for him and they had to tear
me off of him. For a minute I sat
listening then I heard Alex's screams
as they tried to find out where the
resistance's headquarters were. I
knew that Alex could hold out, but if
they didn't get it out of him they
would come and get it out of me. I
knew that I could not hold out
against them if they decided to come
and try to get it out of me. I knew
that Ashley, when she landed at our
headquarters, in Los Angeles, would
send somebody to rescue us. Then

suddenly I thought, if I tell them a lie about where the headquarters are then I could buy Ashley some time. So in an act of self preservation, I yelled, "Stop, stop, wait, I'll tell you where the headquarters are! Just let Alex go, and I'll tell you where it is." Then a Cyclops, who was about seven feet tall, came in and asked angrily, "Where is the headquarters?" I replied quietly, "In New York, in New York. Please let him go, just let him go." Fifteen minutes later, they threw Alex into the room; he was battered and bruised all over. At that moment I swore that they would pay for every bruise, and every cut they put on Alex. I didn't even need to be there when they paid, because eventually they would have to pay. If I didn't make them pay then Ashley would.

IV

Ashley

What do I need to do? Alex and Calypso lost, myself severely injured. When I got to our headquarters in Los Angeles I yelled, "Artemis, Athena, help me get in. I need a little help out here." They replied quickly as one, "We're coming, just give us a minute." After two minutes, they came out helped me inside while I told them what happened. I soon inquired, "Where is Andrew?" "I'm right here." Andrew quietly responded from behind me.

He startled me so much that I fell out of my chair and onto the floor.

To recover from my fall I said, "I need you three to rescue Alex and Calypso. Oh, yeah! Good luck against Medusa." The last sentence I said jokingly but truthfully. They quickly gathered up supplies and left, running out the door. They ran into the desert, and out of sight. They were soon back carrying Alex, who was covered with bruises, and unconscious. Calypso was running swiftly behind them. I quickly placed bandages over his open wounds and placed healing paste on his bruises. He soon awoke and less then fifteen minutes after waking up he sank back into a deep and dreamless sleep that lasted the rest of the night and well into the next day.

In the morning Calypso and I discussed her misadventures in Hera's camp. I was glad that she had thought to lie about where our headquarters are. During the day we both soon became bored, so we decided to go out to gather supplies. During our hunt for supplies in abandoned buildings, we saw Tartarus's hunters and Hera's trackers. They were searching for us, I thought. I was confused, as Calypso had lied and said that our headquarters was in New York. We then realized that they were searching for Zeus, who was neutral, to try and persuade him to their side. We had tried to get him on our side many times, but had always failed. If they could persuade him then the resistance was doomed. When we got back I asked Artemis to find Zeus and persuade him to find another hiding place. What else I need to do, I thought. Then it struck me, what else but to have Artemis to persuade Zeus onto our side.

V

Alex

As I woke up, two days after
Andrew, Artemis, and Athena
rescued Calypso and me, I noticed it
was the afternoon. Then I saw
Ashley, my beloved sister, and
Calypso, the girl that I love, looking
at me with looks full of worry. So I
asked quietly, "Who has died, for
your looks are full of sorrow?" They
all laughed in spite of themselves.
They replied together "No one has
died, but you nearly did." I laughed
at their joke for I knew that had they
not rescued me that I would indeed
be dead. "So," I questioned, "was no

one injured?" My sister said in a voice like silk, "None, except you my misadventurous little brother." They then left me to rest, as even that tiny conversation had worn me out.

As I slept I dreamt of Tartarus getting stronger, he was almost strong enough to overwhelm our measly defenses. When I awoke I told Andrew that his sister Makenzie was coming along with Zethes, who was having second thoughts about not joining the resistance. They're both good warriors, but our combined strength, of the entire resistance, would be enough to capture them to sway them onto our side. Once they were on our side we would be strong enough to overthrow Tartarus and Hera. After they were overthrown we could bring the hidden out of hiding, return the world to a better place, and keep the world from being destroyed by those who wish to destroy it.

VI

Calypso

"Hey, Alex, want to go and get some supplies?" I inquired. "Sure, Calypso, I have been so bored!" Alex exclaimed quickly. After we left we went towards the labyrinth, which is a maze that had once housed the Minotaur. The labyrinth was once said to be unsolvable. As we approached the maze, the Minotaur stepped out of the shadows and tossed us deep into the labyrinth. Soon the Minotaur drew close again laughing. Alex shoved me behind him and told me to run. I immediately took off running as fast as I possibly could. I felt as though I had been running for hours, but I knew that I only ran for minutes. As I drew close to the exit I saw a pure white Pegasus. I jumped upon its back, and I rode it back to headquarters crying the entire way.

When I finally arrived, I quickly ran to my room and cried all night thinking that Alex was dead and that it was entirely my fault. What I didn't know was that Ashley was looking for Alex and me. In the morning, I went back to the labyrinth, going to the center and fighting hydras left and right. I must have killed fifty hydras. It seemed like they didn't want to kill me, but instead wear me down.   When I got to the center, expecting Alex's lifeless body, I got a surprise. Alex wasn't there! I ran back to headquarters feeling absolutely fantastic. I only hoped that whoever saved him was a friend to the resistance.

VII

Ashley

I wonder where Alex and Calypso have gone. I might as well get some supplies as I look for them. "Athena, I'm going out. If Artemis comes back just tell her I went out." I yelled into the room next to mine. I peeked into the next room where Athena had her nose in a book while her hand was flying across a sheet of paper.

As I left, I noticed a strange shadow in the sky. I quickly hurried down the road to the labyrinth. I noticed inside the labyrinth that the Minotaur was laughing at someone.

I hurried inside, and just as I turned a corner, I saw Alex, the fool, trying to stand alone against the Minotaur. I quickly drew my sword and just as the Minotaur bent down to finish off Alex, I chopped off its head. As it disappeared, as monsters do, I said with a sense of finality, "Off with your head." I knew that the Minotaur was not going to be bothering anyone anytime soon. At that note I said quietly to Alex, whom was unconscious, "You know you should really try to stay conscious a lot more, because you weigh quite a bit." As I carried him back to headquarters, I thought where in the lord's name is Calypso? As I thought

more about it I realized that Alex
must have told Calypso to run while
he held off the Minotaur, and then I
realized my brother must have a
crush on Calypso! Now any other
time I would have teased him, but it
was neither the time nor the place
for that. It would not do for me, the
leader of the resistance, to go
around teasing people. Also, I could
always tease him when he woke up.
I am not always as strict as other
leaders, plus siblings tease each
other all the time.

VIII

Alex

When the Minotaur bent over to finish me off, I saw Ashley drawing her sword and preparing to spring at the Minotaur's unprotected neck. As she sprung, I felt the Minotaur's horn cut into my shoulder. When she cut off its head I was immensely grateful, as this stopped it from killing me. Sadly, I did not have time to say such things, as seconds after the thoughts entered my head I fell unconscious.

Slowly as I came back into the real world, after hours of half-formed thoughts, I thought, well I'm not dead after all. Thank you, Ashley.

When I was fully conscious, I was
startled as Calypso had her face right
above my own. I then half-yelled,
"Calypso, get your face out of mine!"
She jerked her head back
murmuring, "Sorry, sorry." I got
stiffly up out of bed and inquired,
"How many days have I been
unconscious?" Ashley held up three
fingers. Amazed, I asked, "Were you
unable to wake me up?" Calypso
nodded, tears streaming down her
face. While I was asleep, Artemis had
come back with Zeus, who had
decided to join our crusade against
Tartarus and Hera. Now the
resistance could begin healing so
that in a few weeks the resistance

could become the downfall of
Tartarus, Hera, and their followers.
Of course, not everyone would want
them to fall, but they will fall
eventually.

IX

Ashley

Now that Alex is no longer unconscious, we can finally begin extensive training for the battle against Tartarus and Hera. Zeus arrived soon before Alex became conscious so we all were able to train for the upcoming battle. We started with swordplay with Jason leading, and then we went into magic with Zeus leading. Zeus said, "We have a really good chance of defeating Tartarus and my treacherous wife, Hera."

After Zeus's lessons on magic I helped them with strategy. After that, Zethes and Makenzie burst in with their swords drawn and were quickly stopped in their tracks by Zeus with a ray of magic. Soon after as they were being interrogated they switched sides and became spies for us. We continued training our minds and bodies for the upcoming battles. We knew even if we overthrew Tartarus and Hera there would still be the few who would be still loyal to them, who were trying to kill us.

X

Calypso

How will I be able to tell Alex that I cannot stand with them against Hera and Tartarus? I must, instead, return to my forgotten island. Although my island is beautiful, full of magical plants, and where I never age, I don't want to ever return to my island. I want to stay here with the resistance forever. So far as I can tell the resident of the island once in a thousand years can leave for three months, and my time away from the island has sadly come to an end. The months I have spent away from the island, though terrifying, have been the best of my life. Now I am supposed to go back to an island that is always forgotten by those who visit it. "Alex," I called, "I need to tell you something. My time here has come to an end. I must return to my home." Alex quickly replied, "Are you still going to leave if I tell you that you are the love of my life?" I said, slowly, "Alex, I'm going to leave no matter what. I do not love you. You would be like extra and useless baggage. You never loved me; you were in love with the idea of love. You will never remember me once I leave. Goodbye, Alex." I then quickly, though left feeling bad; as I had lied to Alex for I really do love him. I knew that one day I would see him again even if I had to travel to the underworld and see him while he was dead. I hoped that I wouldn't have to do this but I figured that I would.

Part Two

To the Fight

XI

Jason

Great, more training with Ashley and Alex. Sadly, Alex is having a lot of trouble concentrating ever since Calypso left. Alex needs to get a grip on the here and now. If he doesn't then he is going to be dying very quickly in the upcoming battles. If he dies on my watch I'll never hear the end of it from Ashley, but back to training. As we were training Alex got the "Deathblow" about forty times. He got about ten bruises and six cuts. I said to him, "Alex, I'm going to give you extra lessons on swordplay." To this he only nodded

7274

making me doubt if he was even listening to me. I then took his hair in my hands, threw him onto the practice mat and began fighting him in hand to hand combat. Normally he would win in about three minutes but today he lost after only a few minutes. I knew that something was wrong. Ashley took him up into her room and talked to him, when she came back she was alone. After she came back she fought harder and better than she ever had before. I praised her for this and she then threw me onto the mat and did the exact same thing that I had done to Alex moments before. Oh the irony. She quickly defeated me, as many do. I truly am terrible at hand to hand combat.

XII

Ares

I am the god of war, carnage, and death. To all my enemies, also known as the resistance, I am known as their doom. Hera, my mother, has not allowed me to attack the puny resistance. So instead I told Medusa and the Minotaur to go and attack the resistance, I told them to have free reign. As they left I felt a little spark of happiness, soon the resistance would be dead and my mother and Tartarus would rule forever. I would not even have to leave my room to watch as the resistance leader, Ashley Brown, was brought to my feet to be killed. Soon I would have completed my one true task in life, to destroy my mortal enemy. She had always escaped until now that is. I truly hoped that the Minotaur and Medusa would be able to capture her without killing her. Sadly, they were my only chance as all the other monsters were afraid of Ashley. They were supposed to be even more afraid of me. Why are they more scared of her? Soon they will be even more scared of me after I kill Ashley, I thought with a cruel smile. I then thought that my mortal enemy should not die quickly, but instead she should die slowly and painfully.

So thus my idea of the hydras torturing her for information, then me killing her was born.

XIII

Ashley

After I talked to Alex I sent him to the infirmary where I hoped they would be able to help him move on from Calypso. Sadly I was wrong; three days after I sent him there a nurse came and told me that Alex was dead. I went to go and see him. I gasped when I saw him. His cheeks were sunken and hollow, his eyes open, and his frame limp, slight, and tiny. He looked awful. I admit it; I did not want to accept the fact that my brother was dead. I missed him immediately. I never want to go through something like that again. A few minutes after entering the infirmary where Alex was, Medusa and the Minotaur attacked. I grabbed my sword from where it was leaning against the wall and in a fury went into the courtyard and attacked the attacking monsters. I was like a demon; no monster could escape me once I decided to kill it. I laughed a crazy laugh that even scared me once or twice. Then I saw my old enemy, the Minotaur. I sneaked up behind it and for the second time in a month chopped off its head. It then disappeared and moments later I was knocked out from behind, by Medusa. She dragged me off back to Hera's camp where, when I was awake, I was thrown at my mortal enemy's feet. My mortal enemy is Hera's son, Ares.

XIV

Jason

As I saw Ashley jump out into the battle, I saw that she was like a demon. She was beautiful in a terrifying sort of way, with her eyes blazing with fury she really did look like a gorgeous demon. She was killing everything in her path. She chopped off the Minotaur's head, again. She was, at the end of the battle, knocked out by Medusa. Medusa then dragged her off with me following cautiously. When I saw that Ares was in Hera's camp, where Medusa headed, I faltered for only a moment. Ares had quite a fearsome reputation in the resistance. He was the model warrior, strong, brave, and fearless. I felt a rage at the thought of him killing Ashley. I then realized that I had a crush on her. Oh great, this was bad! The resistance in chaos, Ashley captured, and Alex dead. This day was turning out to be a very bad day. If this day could be redone then I would have immediately cut off Medusa's head. Well at least I know why Medusa and the Minotaur attacked us. Now I also know who I have to defeat to get Ashley back. I, sadly, would have preferred not to have known. Too bad, I thought, I'm going to save her, have her fall in love with me, and

then we would find a way to defeat
Hera and Tartarus. Why couldn't I
have been born a mortal?

XV

Ares

"Medusa, status report" I ordered. "Sir, I am the only one who will be coming back from the battle. All the others were killed by Ashley Brown. I only survived because I hit her in the head from behind." said Medusa. "Good, good. Hydras, torture Ashley until she begs for mercy, until she begs to be killed. Send for me when she begs to be killed. I want to have the pleasure of killing her myself." I said, in a booming voice. The hydras replied frightened, "We shall do as you command." They took Ashley, who was struggling weakly, into another room where minutes later I heard her screams. I thought that if anyone wished to save her then they needed to come out now. I smiled with glee at that thought. I knew that they would have to go through me, and that was something only Ashley had ever accomplished and even she can't do that without a sword or dagger. I thought that for sure she was going to die. Oh what fun I will have when I kill her, oh what fun.

XVI

Ashley

When I came to, I was in Hera's camp. I heard Ares planning to kill me. I began struggling weakly against the Hydras who were holding me. Ares then said, his voice full of glee, "Torture her until she begs for mercy, until she begs to be killed. Send for me when she begs to be killed. I want the pleasure of killing her myself." I was taken into another room where they began blasting me with fire. I couldn't hold back my screams of agony. Then I couldn't believe it, the hydras stopped!

I opened my eyes and saw Jason standing right in front of me. He had killed the hydras who were torturing me. He then cut off my bonds and gave me my favorite sword. I then whispered, "Thank you." and gave him a kiss on the cheek. We fought our way out of there, and ironically instead of killing Medusa I hit her in the back of the head, knocking her unconscious. As we passed Ares I cut him across his face with the edge of my sword. I knew that he would have preferred to die rather than be wounded by me, again. I couldn't hold back my glee at the thought so I smiled my old, happy smile from when I didn't know I was a demigod.

For once, I was happy with our chances. As we left I thought, take that Hera.

XVII

Jason

As we left Ashley was so beautiful, even though she was covered in soot, cut and burned, and with her clothes burnt and hanging in tatters. Then as we passed along a cliff, Tartarus stepped out of the shadows and pushed Ashley off the cliff. As she fell Ares jumped, caught her, set her down safely, and then ran off. I then slowly climbed down to where she was and helped her back up the side of the cliff. All the time I was wondering why Ares saved her. Why? We then half walked, half jogged back to headquarters. When

we got there everyone was worried.
Ashley was sent to the infirmary for
her burns and I got chewed out by
Artemis. How is that fair, I saved
Ashley. I should be getting a medal,
but, no, instead I get chewed out.

While I was getting chewed out, I
asked, "Artemis has anyone heard
from Makenzie or Zethes?" With
tears in her eyes Artemis replied,
"Ares found out that they were spies
and he killed them. Andrew is
heartbroken over the loss of his
sister." I went to Andrew's room,
hoping to cheer him up, and said to
him, "Makenzie died with honor. She
probably fought till the end."
Andrew replied sadly, "I hope so, and

knowing her that is probably true." I left knowing that that simple visit had left Andrew in a better mood then he had been in.

XVIII

Ares

Five minutes after the battle
where Ashley cut me across my face
and escaped me once again, I saw
Tartarus push her off a cliff. I
jumped, caught her, laid her safely
on the ground, and then I ran. While
I ran I thought about why I saved
her. Then I realized, she could have
killed me but she didn't so I was in
her debt. Now since I saved her I am
no longer.

Then Tartarus stepped out of the
shadows, and pushed me over the
cliff's edge and into the endless
cavern that was beside me. As I fell I

thought why do I hate being in someone's debt. If I didn't hate being in someone's dept, and if I had not saved her, then I would not be falling for the rest of eternity. I thought that I would fall bored out of my mind for the rest of eternity. I saw then that there were monsters falling at a slower pace than I was, so when I saw one I killed it. I decided to do this until the end of time.

XIX

Ashley

When I was finished in the infirmary, we began suiting up. We were suiting up in our armor so that we could invade Hera's camp and overthrow Hera and Tartarus. When we were finished suiting up everyone got on a Pegasus and we flew towards Hera's camp. Around three hours later we arrived. We set down in a clearing about a mile away from the camp. When we got there we sent our Pegasus into the camp to cause a distraction. As the distraction began we all ran into the camp slaying every monster there.

As we fought I noticed that, strangely, the monsters were not trying to kill us, instead they were trying to wound us so we couldn't fight. Medusa and Ares were, strangely, absent from the battle. I fought beside Jason at the front. During the battle we must have killed dozens of Hydras and Cyclops.

Soon all the monsters were dead and when Tartarus and Hera put up a fight and wounded Artemis, slightly, they were disarmed and overthrown. We sent them into the Arctic so that they could bother anyone else and so that no one could bother them. We were kind enough as to not kill them, but they seemed to think that the Arctic was a fate worse than death. So be it, I guess.

When we, finally, finished cleaning up from the battle we began walking back to our headquarters. Along the way Medusa stepped out of the shadows and, for the second time in a day, I was pushed off the cliff. Jason hopped on a nearby Pegasus and saved me from dying. I was saved from dying by two different guys in the same day. What a sorry excuse for a hero I am. When we got to the top he stepped off and was about to help me down from the Pegasus when Medusa whipped off her sunglasses and turned him into a statue. I took my sword out from its sheathe and cut off her head. I then stood crying as I beheld the statue that was once Jason. I called out to the others that Jason was dead and that I no longer wished to be a leader. I told them that I wished for Andrew to become the leader, and that I wanted to find Calypso and live with her on her island. I left and I never saw them again, until a fateful day when I would be needed once again.

XX

Ashley

Two years later I found Calypso's island, where she welcomed me with open arms. I told her of what had happened the past years. We spent three days crying over the loss of the ones that we loved. When finally we no longer cried over them, I said to her, "I want to stay here with you until I die." She made me an immortal so that I could stay with her forever. I never forgot Jason's face, but I did not cry over him again until I met a boy who looked just like him. I learned the boy's name. It was Marcus, and he also is a son of

Athena. Like all the others he left Calypso's island in due time. I ran away from them, and until he was gone only Calypso saw me.

Sadly, now I cry over Jason's death every day and I probably will. I knew that Medusa would one day come back to life. Medusa will come back knowing that I was immortal. She would come to me looking for revenge, but she will not find it. Each time when she comes back I will cut off her head again and again. I will feel no joy at doing this; instead I will feel as though I am getting revenge over Jason's death. I will always remember the resistance and what happened in the days we tried to overthrow Tartarus and Hera. Maybe one day I will return to the resistance and help them with the democratic government that they plan on setting up for the mythical realm.

Part Three

Back to the Modern World

XXI

Andrew

Soon after the battle we all saw Ashley get pushed off of a cliff by Medusa and Jason catching her. Five minutes later we heard Ashley shout, "Jason is dead. Andrew, I nominate you to become the new leader of the resistance. I'm going to find Calypso and go live with her." We saw her fly off on a Pegasus into the sky and we knew that we wouldn't be seeing her for a long time.

A few days later I was elected to be the new president of the mythical realm. I did my best but without Ashley's help, I must admit, I was quite incompetent with the workings of the democratic government. I sent out Athena, Artemis, and Zeus out to find Ashley, but I knew that they wouldn't find her. I sent Iris messages, about a hundred, but they never could contact her. She knew I never wanted to lead, so why choose me?

I hoped every day that she would change her mind and come home. I knew that as long as Ashley was grieving over Jason's death she wouldn't come home but I still hoped and sent out search parties. I knew that they would never find her; Ashley was too smart to be found.

Over the years the number of attacks on the government headquarters increased quite a bit. I knew that one day Ashley would decide to come back, I just didn't know when. I had hopes that it was soon, though.

XXII

Ashley

I knew I would have to go back but it wasn't until Calypso showed me how much trouble Andrew was in that I decided to go back. So many people were revolting, I knew Andrew, Zeus, Athena, and Artemis wouldn't be able to hold them back. So I grabbed my armor and ran to Calypso. When I got to Calypso I said, "I need you to build me a boat." Calypso nodded and in a snap of her fingers a magic boat appeared. I jumped on and turned the boat towards America.

As I approached the shore I began to wonder what new inventions that I would face in the new day and age. I knew that the world had created the alternative to oil, coal, and natural gas. I also knew that because I was a demigod I would not have any need for it. Then before I could think any more I landed on the shore of San Francisco. It had changed so much. All the buildings were made of glass and reflected back the sunlight. The roofs were made of solar panels. It looked absolutely amazing.

XXIII

Artemis

When I noticed Ashley on the magic boat, nearing the shore of San Francisco, I sent for Andrew because I knew that he would want to meet Ashley as soon as she landed on the shore. I sent Athena to go find Andrew as I thought Ashley shouldn't bother with my plan for killing Andrew; in fact she could be a good partner for my plan.

Then I thought, no she would only be a danger because she will do anything to keep the balance of the mythical realm. She would also not be too keen on letting Tartarus and

Hera come back, but if I can figure out her weakness I can blackmail her into helping me.

I said quietly to Athena, "I'm going on an errand. Tell Andrew that I will be home around ten p.m. tonight." Then I left, but instead of doing something for Andrew I went down into the dark, dank Underworld so that I could take over the demigod resistance. With that thought I felt an evil smile on my lips.

XXIV

Andrew

Athena burst into my office and grabbed me, dragging me into the courtyard where I saw Ashley on a magic raft drifting towards the shore. I jumped for joy, because Ashley was coming to help me with all the problems of running a democracy.

I ran down to the shore, jogged into the ocean and dragged her raft onto the beach. I told her, "Go get some rest and see me when you have had a nap, a meal, and a little training." I also told her to take any room she wanted.

A few hours later she came into my office and asked if there was anything that I needed her to do. I asked her if she knew where Artemis went and Ashley said that she thought that Artemis went to the underworld. I asked her how she knew that, and she replied that she saw Artemis climbing aboard a ship going to the underworld. I jumped up from my desk and walked over to her with a shocked expression on my face. I couldn't imagine why Artemis would go into the underworld. Nor could I imagine Artemis leaving without telling me but I knew Ashley wouldn't lie to me about this.

XXV

Ashley

After I had my nap I was too restless to wait until I had eaten to see Andrew. On my way to see Andrew I spotted Artemis grabbing a spot on the last boat to the underworld. I knew that I should ask whether Andrew knew if Artemis had went to the underworld though why she would go there was beyond me.

I went and talked to Andrew about Artemis and I realized that she shouldn't have had a reason to go to the underworld, unless.....she wanted to find out a person's weakness. I shuddered at that thought; surely she wouldn't have a need to do that. Right? Unless she was wanted to turn traitor to the entire demigod resistance. Which I really hoped would never happen. Though if it did happen someone would have to kill her and I didn't know if even I could do that. May the gods help us if that does happen?

XXVI

Artemis

When I arrived in the underworld I sought out Hades. I asked Hades what Ashley's weaknesses were, but he could not tell me without seeing her in person, so I decided to settle with getting her fears. I employed Hades to give me Phobos, the god of fear, to help me take Ashley down. Hades was more than happy to help me.

When I told him of my plan, he eagerly responded, "I do not wish to allow Ashley to go free. She has been a thorn in my side ever since she was born. I will be happy to see her soul enter my kingdom so that I may torture her in the Fields of Punishment." As he said the final word he laughed an evil, devious laugh. I quickly told him to take his dark, mysterious forces and attack the demigod government center.

I told Hades to destroy whoever he wanted but that I needed Andrew, Ashley, and Athena alive. If they died I would never be able to take over this world. Also if they died I told Hades that I would kill him. Though how I have no idea. He said, There is no need to attack they are coming here. They're after you."

XXVII

Andrew

When Ashley told me of her belief that Artemis was not to be trusted, I believed her because Ashley no matter what tries her hardest to only get true information to the leaders that she sponsors. I trust Ashley with my life. I asked her to go to the underworld to find Artemis, but Ashley politely declined and she said, "The first thing Artemis will do is to get Hades onto her side and I am not about to go fight Hades in his own environment." I decided to respect her choice.

I asked Athena to go but she too said no, though she didn't say no as politely as Ashley. I decided that I would have to go and face Hades myself though I knew that I had no chance of beating him. When Ashley saw me preparing to go to the underworld she asked where I was going, and I replied, "I am going to the very place you will not dare venture to, the underworld." Ashley replied, her voice full of anger and shock, "If you go there you will be killed as soon as you step foot into that awful place, but if you insist on going I will go with you as your bodyguard. I will not do anything except protect you from Hades minions." I nodded because I knew that if I was going Ashley would have no choice but to come too.

I told her to pack her bags and to be ready to go at dawn. She left quickly, knowing that a new war had come. As she left I thought who better to lead this war besides the very person who ended the last one. I didn't know it then but if Ashley hadn't come I would be dog chow in a few hours. Go figure, right?

XXVIII

Ashley

Oh, what have I gotten myself into? Why does Andrew always think I have the answer? Just because I'm the daughter of Athena doesn't mean I always can find the right answer. I quickly got to my room, but because I had to be ready by dawn I couldn't think I could only pack. When I finished packing I wondered if I would ever see this room again. When dawn came I was waiting in the courtyard for Andrew who brought me out a surprise. He had saved my favorite sword from the spot where I had thrown it just moments after taking off Medusa's head.

When I took my sword from his hand I suddenly started crying. I ended up delaying our departure till half past six. When we finally went on our way I was strengthened by the fact that I could find Jason's soul in the underworld, but I was hesitant. I felt as though I wouldn't find him there. I began to wonder if there was in fact a cure for Medusa's gaze. If there was could I save Jason?

Dang it. In my wishful thinking I had gotten behind Andrew. I hastened my pace, but I had no need to worry. Andrew had stopped at the edge of the river Styx. I asked him if he had a gold dollar or anything with even a small bit of gold. He said he had a gold watch so I took it and threw it into the river. Andrew at first began arguing with me, and then he realized that I was correct all I had to do to get us across was to get the ferryman some kind of gold.

I saw the ferryman bring his boat to the shore and I pushed Andrew in and jumped in. I knew that if I had wasted any time he would take his boat without us on it. I told Andrew that we had to be careful. I asked him if he had a bow, but he didn't have one. I couldn't blame him, I had forgotten mine too.

XXIX

Artemis

I have big hopes for my plan. If this plan didn't work then I was so dead. I told Hades that I needed water from the river Styx and that I needed it in a bronze jar. When Hades brought the water to me I took it and cut my palm allowing a few drops of my immortal blood to soak into the water. When my blood had mixed in I poured the water over the statue that had once been Jason Holly. When I stepped back Jason was once again flesh and blood.

While Jason was returning from the realm of stone I tied him up. I wondered how surprised Ashley would be when she sees Jason alive when she cried over him while he was a statue. I was amazed. Perhaps the witch, Circe, truly has divine powers. She did give me the cure for Medusa's gaze so perhaps she does.

I can't wait until I reveal that I have Jason. I wonder how far Ashley will go to have him back. I guess I will just have to wait and see. This is going to be a fun time.

XXX

Andrew

When we got in the underworld
Ashley turned and started running as
though her life depended on it.
When I caught up with her she
screamed, "I heard him. I heard
Jason! He must be alive!" She ran
straight at a solid brick wall, and she
ran straight through it. Well, I
thought it was solid.

I charged in after her. When I got
in I saw the Minotaur. Well Ashley
will take care of him, and then I saw
Jason. He was sitting there tied up.
Ashley was standing in front of him

crying. "Ashley. Ashley. Ashley!" he yelled.

She collapsed, and then everything turned black. When I woke up I realized that we were in a cave and I also realized that Ashley was nowhere to be seen, but Jason was in front of me. I tried talking to Jason, but he was unconscious. I tested my bonds to see if I could get out of them. I couldn't break them. If only I could break free I would be able to get us out of here.

XXXI

Ashley

As we stepped out of the boat I heard a whisper. It sounded like Jason! I took off running. In my way was a brick wall. I was determined to get to the other side of that wall. I ran straight at the wall and, to my great surprise, straight through it.

When I got through I saw the Minotaur and Jason. I ran forward stopping right in front of him not believing my eyes. I couldn't stop myself. I whispered "I thought you were dead." I started crying. Then moments later I felt dizzy.

Everything went black and I felt my nose crunch as I hit the floor.

When I woke up I was staring into the face of Hades, my second worst enemy. I knew I had blood all over my face but I didn't care so I spat into his face but he just laughed. Then he stepped back and I saw Artemis, free and just standing there. In an instant I knew that she was a traitor so I screamed, "Why, Artemis, why? I guess all rabid dogs turn to bite the hand that feeds them." Artemis stepped forward and slapped me, but instead of getting angry I just laughed. Moments later I saw Phobos, the god of fear, step into the light. I was terrified of that guy, honestly I do not know a person alive who can stand him except for Hades but I don't count him as a person. If Phobos was there though what did they need me for?

XXXII

Artemis

When Ashley woke up I was waiting behind Hades, and when he stepped aside Ashley yelled, "Why, Artemis, why? I guess all rabid dogs bite the hand that feeds them." I stepped forward and slapped her, hard. I motioned Phobos forward. I watched Ashley turn pale at the sight of him and I smiled.

I motioned for Hades to follow me out and leave Ashley with Phobos who would get all the information I needed. When I got out of that room and Hades stood in front of me he said, "I thought that

you said I could kill her!" I replied,
"You will get to kill her as soon as I
get the results that I want." After I
said that Hades sulked away. I knew
I would get what I wanted and I
didn't want Hades to kill Ashley, my
master wanted to have that pleasure
himself. I followed Hades, quietly,
and when no one else was around I
killed him with the knife Circe sent
me that could kill any immortal.

XXXIII

Andrew

I woke up startled, because I didn't know where I was. Then I remembered the events of the past day. I looked around and saw Jason sitting across from me; he was tied up from head to toe. I wiggled and found that my bounds were loose. It took me a while but I finally slipped out of them and walked over to Jason taking off his bounds. I said, "We have to get out of here and find Ashley before we do anything else." Jason nodded to me once then he took off running towards the northeast exit. He ran through the hallways as though he knew exactly where he was going. At the end of a really long hallway there was a door that was slightly open. I looked through the opening and say Ashley laying on the floor in a faint. Her nose was also broken and her face was covered in dried blood. I was stunned; Ashley never faints unless she is scared beyond compare. Whatever scared her terrifies me.

I said to Jason in a whisper, "Ashley looks fine but she has fainted and has a broken nose." Jason walked over to me and looked at Ashley. He looked around to see if there was a weapon nearby and he saw an abandoned sword lying near the wall. He motioned to me that I should open the door on the count of three. He mouthed one, two, three and I flung open the door where we saw Phobos standing above Ashley. I stood there starring while Jason charged at Phobos alone. I watched as Jason cut Phobos across his chest before he could even draw his sword. Incredibly instead of fighting Phobos disappeared in a plume of red smoke. Jason said to me, "Help me carry Ashley so we can get out of this place." I walked over to Ashley and with her between us we got her out of the underworld and back to my house. When we got there I warned

everybody to watch out for Artemis,
that she was no longer our ally.
Then with Jason at my side I waited
for Ashley to wake up.

XXXIV

Ashley

When Artemis and Hades left the room I was more scared than I had ever been in my entire life. So I did the only logical thing I could think of, I fainted. When I woke back up I saw Jason, Andrew, and Athena sitting in the room. I figured out that I was back in the real world at Andrew's house. I got up and said, "I know who Artemis is working for." I got everyone's attention with that statement. I took a deep breath and continued, "She is working for Hera and Tartarus. It is time for them to be killed." After I told them that little speech I walked out and got my armor on and found my favorite sword. When I got back to my room nobody had moved so I decided to yell at them, "Do you think we can beat them by sitting around? Go get on your armor and meet me in the courtyard in five minutes. Now go and get ready for battle!" They immediately scattered, running as fast as they could.

When I got to the courtyard they were all there and ready so I told them to get a boat because we were taking a trip to the Arctic. On our way to the Arctic we only stopped twice. The first time we stopped was to help some demigods who were fighting rebels who were against Andrew, and the second time we stopped to kill some hydras. We finally got to the Arctic and since it was in the summer it was a rather moderate temperature for the Arctic.

I went ahead and spotted Hera walking with Tartarus. I grabbed my bow and notched an arrow. I aimed it at Tartarus and loosed the arrow. It flew straight and true but Tartarus grabbed Hera and moved her so that she was killed instead of him. I ran knowing that he knew someone was there.

I ran back to the others and told them what happened. I told them that we had to hurry and hide before Tartarus came. I told them that he was too powerful for us to beat on our own. I heard Tartarus coming so I told them to hide. I led Tartarus away from everyone else and when he was close enough I stabbed him through the heart with my sword. I felt a sharp pain in my side and when I looked down I saw that he had stabbed me right beneath my ribs with a knife. As he died he whispered, "If I'm going to die I'm taking you with me." I quickly pushed him away.

Holding my side I ran back to the others as fast as I could but before I could get halfway back to them I started to see black spots in my vision and I knew I was about to pass out from blood loss. I barely got back to the others before I passed out. When I woke back up I was in a bed in the infirmary of Andrew's house.

I decided not to wait until someone came to see if I was awake, so I got up stiffly and walked to the dining room where Andrew and Jason were talking. They didn't notice me so I said, "Are you two going to ignore me all night?" They turned around to see who had spoken and when they saw me they had grins on their faces. Then they looked a little sad. I must have had a confused look on my face because Jason said in a voice barely above a whisper, "Artemis found us and wounded Athena and we don't know if she is going to make it." I turned and ran to the infirmary when I heard this information. I saw only one door closed so I walked to it and opened the door and went inside.

When I got inside I saw Athena wrapped up in gauze and linen and I knew that she wasn't going to make it. I walked out crying and told everyone I was going back to Calypso's island where I would stay till the end of my life. I told them never to bother and that if they did I would kill whoever came after me.

They knew that I wasn't joking about them sending anyone so when I left Andrew sent no one to talk to me. To this day I remain with Calypso on her island, tending to the demigods who find their way there with her. Though unlike Calypso, who helps them heal, I help them practice their swordsmanship and fighting skills. The only time I will return to the civilized world is when I am dead and that will be for me to be buried at the Demigod Resistance's old headquarters in Los Angeles.

Glossary

Athena- goddess of wisdom and knowledge

Ares- god of war

Artemis- goddess of hunting and archer

Demigod- a son or daughter of a god or goddess

Hades- god of the dead

Hera- goddess of the home and marriage and wife to Zeus

Hydras- seven headed dragon whose middle head shoots fire and the other heads spit acid

Medusa- a gorgon whose stare turns any living thing to stone

Minotaur- half man half bull

Phobos- son of Ares and the god of fear

Tartarus- god of the pit and darkness

Zeus- god of magic and husband to Hera

DISCARD

Made in the USA
Lexington, KY
02 February 2015